Walter the Whistler Bear

Written by KATHLEEN SHERIDAN RUSSELL
Illustrated by LUCY WATSON

A heartfelt thanks to:

Lindsay, Cameron, and Kenneth for their grammatical and poetic expertise, unwavering support, and immense patience:

Barbara for encouraging me to finish and share Alasdair's story about Walter:

and Lucy for her artistic talent, enthusiasm, and commitment to creating images that matched Alasdair's vision.

Kathleen Sheridan Russell

To create Walter the Whistler Bear together was a treasured experience, Kathleen. Thank you. Walter's story will remind us of the cherished good times with the Russell family in Whistler.

Lucy Watson

Walter the Whistler Bear

~ Inspired by Alasdair Cairns Russell ~

Up high in the mountains lived Walter the Cub,

Who **awoke** from his sleep and needed some **grub**.

Walter's **tummy** was **rumbling**, he had to be hasty,

So he followed his **nose**, off to find something **tasty**.

Walter had visions of
pizza, noodles, and fries,
As he sped down the slopes while **shutting** his eyes.

Outside of the **village**, he found such a **feast**;
Walter **jumped in the truck** and ate like a beast.

Once the cub was quite full, from his head to his toes,
He made himself comfy and lay down for a doze.

From **mountains** to **city** the garbage truck **sped,**
While **snoozing** inside was our **Whistler ted.**

With a **shudder** and a **stop**, the trip came to an end,
Walter leapt out in surprise to go look for a friend.

Stanley Park was **abuzz** with guests sitting on chairs,

But **none** of them wanted to make friends with **stray bears.**

Walter then
spotted someone
under a tree,

It was a boy and his bear
whom he'd called Ted E.

With his new friends,
Walter's spirits were brightened,

But the visitors around were still
all quite frightened.

The trio then hid with their chums from the sea,

Hoping no one would notice
Walter, The Boy, and Ted E.

The Boy quickly realized they needed a plan,

So he thought of a place which liked bears more than man.

Getting inside was not easily done,
But our trio was determined to search for some fun.

There were bears dressed like clowns, a hero, and a fairy,
Looking really quite happy and not nearly so scary.

They all jumped in surprise when Walter hit the first key
And were truly impressed by how musical he could be.

Dressed up as a hero, Walter slipped into the crowd;

Then our friends went **sightseeing** where bears aren't allowed.

The chums spent the day exploring the town,

And headed to
the mall to wolf
a snack down.

Then back to the park went the adventurous three,
Now everyone knew how fun bear cubs could be.

Alas, all good days must come to an end,
Walter knew that he must say goodbye to his friend.

Walter spotted the truck that had brought him to town,
And he hopped back inside to have a lie down.

As the truck bumpety-bumped and sped on its way,
Walter thought of The Boy he'd made friends
with that day.

He arrived at his **home** with the mountains *aglow*,

While cherishing the friends he had gotten to know.

Walter quietly climbed back into his cave,

for a special friend

Where he realized with **good friends**, he could always be **brave**.

KATHLEEN SHERIDAN RUSSELL learned what sorts of adventures appeal to children during more than 20 years of family holidays in Whistler. Kathleen's family includes her son Cameron, her daugther Lindsay, two lovable dogs, and a crazy cat. This is her first book.

LUCY WATSON lives in the United Kingdom and has enjoyed family holidays in Whistler and Vancouver. She is passionate about encouraging children to seek out new experiences and believes that amusing illustrations can help pave the way (perhaps along with a snack or two!).

ALASDAIR CAIRNS RUSSELL, at age 14, read an article about a bear cub in Whistler that fell asleep in a garbage truck and awoke in Vancouver. Alasdair was relieved to learn that the cub was safely returned home, but he wondered what the bear actually did in the big city. From this premise, Alasdair created Walter the Whistler Bear, a lovable cheeky cub who had a fun day exploring Vancouver. Kathleen and Lucy took inspiration from Alasdair's original ideas and artwork to craft Walter's story.

 FriesenPress

Suite 300 - 990 Fort St
Victoria, BC, V8V 3K2
Canada

www.friesenpress.com

Illustrated by Lucy Watson

ISBN
978-1-03-910667-3 (Hardcover)
978-1-03-910666-6 (Paperback)
978-1-03-910668-0 (eBook)

1. JUVENILE FICTION, ANIMALS, BEARS

Distributed to the trade by The Ingram Book Company

CPSIA information can be obtained
at www.ICGtesting.com
Printed in the USA
BVHW060009300921
617775BV00002B/55

9 781039 106673